Holiday House · New York

VALERI GORBACHEV

Lost and Found Ducklings

A package arrived for Brother Duck and Sister Duck.
What could be inside?
A train set?
No.
A dollhouse?
No.
A bicycle?
No.

"Peep!" said Brother Duck. "Nets!"
"Peep!" said Sister Duck. "Let's catch things!"

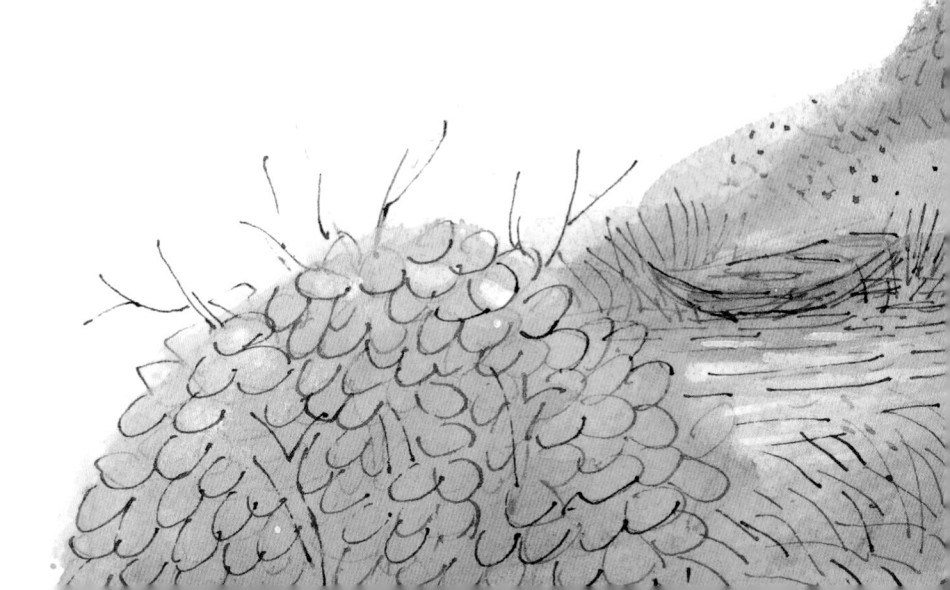

"Quack," said Mama Duck. "Stay close to home."
"Quack," said Papa Duck. "Don't get lost."

"Peep! We will," said Sister Duck.
"Peep! We won't," said Brother Duck.

"Look! A butterfly!" said Sister Duck.
"Let's catch it," said Brother Duck.
"It got away," said Sister Duck.

"It got away," said Sister Duck.

"Look! A frog!" said Sister Duck.
"Let's catch it," said Brother Duck.

"Let's go home," said Sister Duck.
"Okay," said Brother Duck.
"Which way do we go?" said Sister Duck.

From up above came a sharp

Hooooooot! Hoooooot!

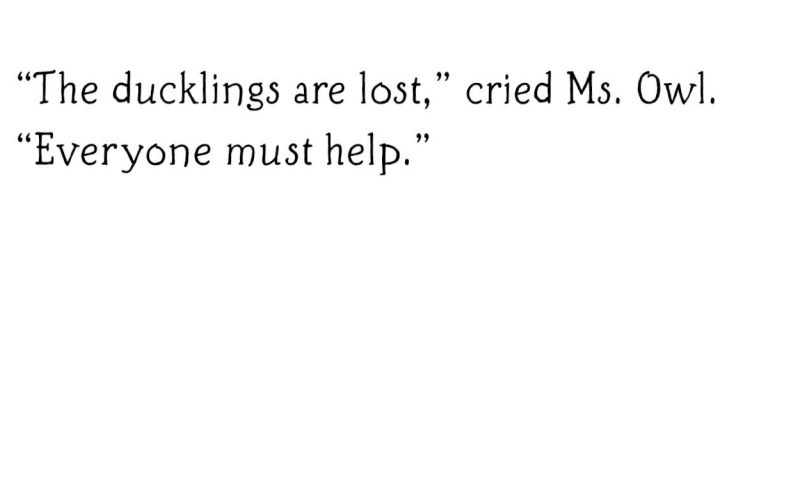

"The ducklings are lost," cried Ms. Owl.
"Everyone must help."

"Your Mama and Papa will come when they hear my earthshaking bellow," said Mr. Moose.

MOOOOOOOOO!

MOOOOOOOOO!

Mr. Moose's moo was truly earthshaking,
but Mama and Papa Duck did not come.

The ducklings cried . . .

Peep!   Peep!   Peep!

"Your Mama and Papa will come when they hear my piercing howl," said Ms. Wolf.

Awooooooooo!
Awoooooooooo!

Ms. Wolf's call was piercing indeed, but Mama and Papa Duck did not come.

The ducklings cried . . .

Peep! Peep! Peep!

"Your Mama and Papa will come when they hear my shrill scream," said Ms. Fox.

Eeeeeeeeek!
Eeeeeeeeek!

But Mama and Papa Duck did not come.

The ducklings cried . . .

Peep! Peep! Peep!

"Your Mama and Papa will come when they hear my fierce growl," said Mr. Bear.

Grrrrrrrrrr! Grrrrrrrrrr!

But Mama and Papa Duck still
did not come.

The ducklings cried . . .

Peep!   Peep!   Peep!

Poor Brother Duck! Poor Sister Duck! They cried and they peeped, and they peeped and they cried.

Ms. Owl hooted, Mr. Moose bellowed, Ms. Wolf howled, Ms. Fox screamed, and Mr. Bear growled. The forest had become a very noisy place.

Grrrrrrrrrr!

Eeeeeeeeek! Eeeeeeeeek!

It was so noisy that the ducklings could barely hear . . .

Quack quack quack!   Quack quack quack!
Quack quack quack!   Quack quack quack!

Mother Duck came running.   Father Duck came running.

"Did you hear my earthshaking bellow?" asked Mr. Moose.
"Did you hear my piercing howl?" asked Ms. Wolf.
"My shrill scream?" asked Ms. Fox.
"My fierce growl?" asked Mr. Bear.
"Hoot!" said Ms. Owl.

"What we heard," said Mama Duck, "was the sweet peep-peep-peep of our dear little ducklings . . . the mightiest sound of all."

For my daughter, Sasha

Library of Congress Cataloging-in-Publication Data

Names: Gorbachev, Valeri, author, illustrator.
Title: Lost and found ducklings / Valeri Gorbachev.
Description: First edition. | New York : Holiday House, [2019] | Summary:
"Sister Duck and Brother Duck are lost, so all of the animals use their
biggest hoots, bellows, howls, and growls to summon Mama and Papa"—
Provided by publisher.
Identifiers: LCCN 2018002100 | ISBN 9780823441075 (hardcover)
Subjects: | CYAC: Lost children—Fiction. | Ducks—Fiction.
Animals—Infancy—Fiction. | Forest animals—Fiction. | Animal sounds—Fiction.
Classification: LCC PZ7.G6475 Los 2019 | DDC [E]—dc23 LC record available
at https://lccn.loc.gov/2018002100